To little Miguel, so he can forever live surrounded with books and love.
Rafael Ordóñez

To Clarisa, for sharing this jungle adventure with me.
César Barceló

BananaNow
Somos8 Series

© Text: Rafael Ordóñez, 2025
© Illustrations: César Barceló, 2025
© Edition: NubeOcho, 2025
© English translation: Cecilia Ross, 2025
www.nubeocho.com · hello@nubeocho.com

Original Title: *Telebanana*
Text editing: Caroline Dookie, Rebecca Packard, Robin Sinclair

First edition: September, 2025
ISBN: 978-84-10406-41-4
Legal Deposit: M-2386-2025

Printed in Slovenia.

All rights reserved. Reproduction is strictly prohibited.

BananaNow

Rafael Ordóñez   César Barceló

In the jungle, everything had become very modern and high-tech.

The animals were always online, glued to their phones, their tablets, their computers, and their video game consoles.

Hippo played online games with Crocodile, who lived two rivers over.

Queen Ant used her map app to find the right path back to the anthill.

Giraffe was busy chatting on her computer—even with the animals close by!

Gorilla practiced strange poses for unique selfies.

The jungle creatures weren't swimming and playing in the river, they weren't stopping to enjoy the afternoon breeze, they weren't smiling... They were acting like robots!

Some of them were even forgetting that they needed to eat!

One afternoon, Hippo's stomach let out a strange grumbling that was so loud, it sounded like a leopard growling...

And that gave Monkey an idea!

If the animals were too busy to find food, he'd deliver it straight to their doors!

And who knows? He might even make a fortune along the way!

"Listen here, big fellow," said Monkey.

Hippo didn't move, he just kept right on playing his video game.

Monkey flipped over so that his head was blocking the screen.

"Aren't you hungry, Hippo? What would you say to some nice fresh lettuce? A peanut pizza? A cauliflower yogurt?"

"If you help me, I'll give you a Swiss chard sandwich with pineapple."

Hippo shut his eyes tight, imagining all that tasty food.

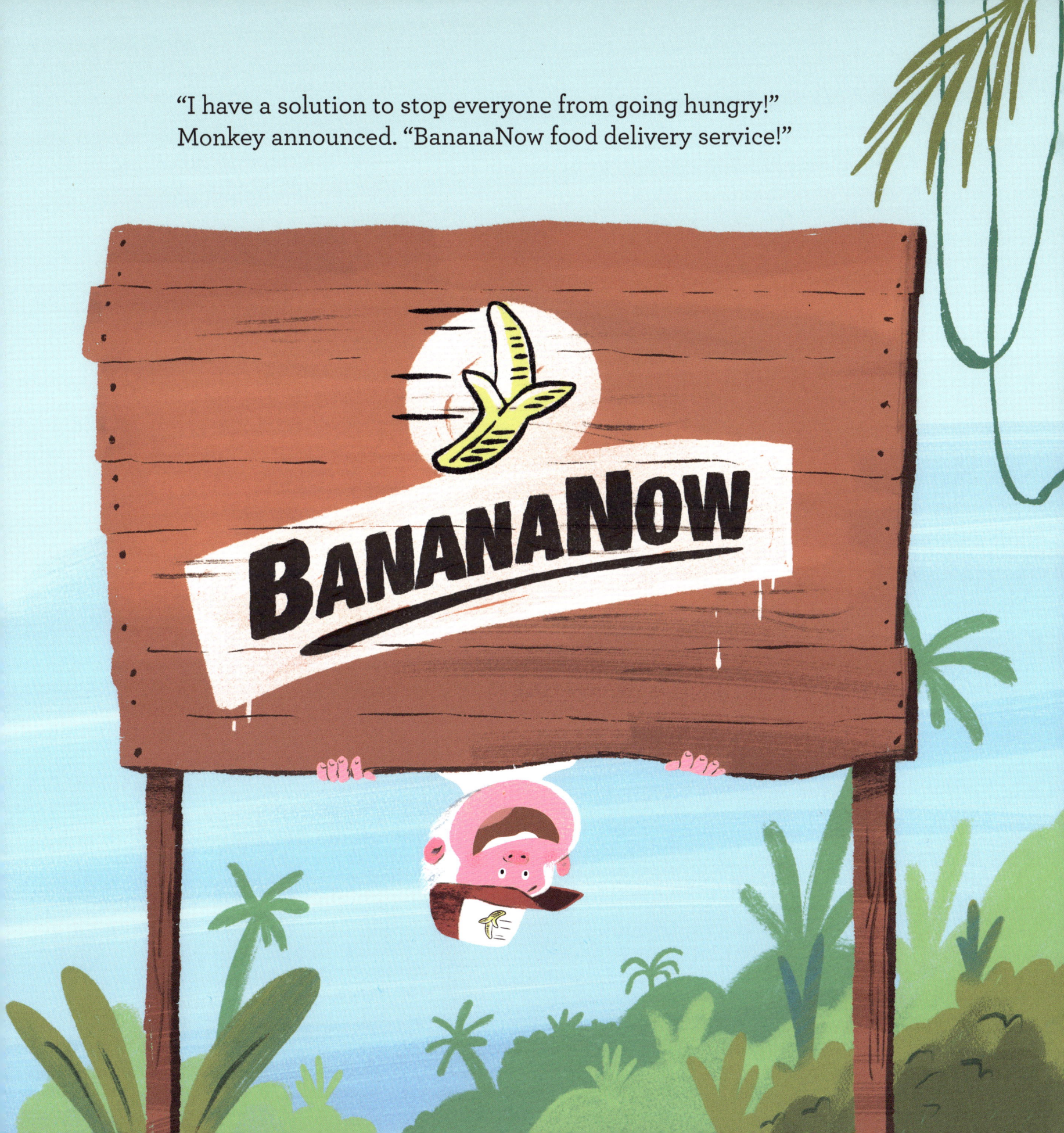

"I have a solution to stop everyone from going hungry!" Monkey announced. "BananaNow food delivery service!"

Hippo started helping and texted all his contacts on social media. In a matter of minutes, every animal in the jungle knew they could order their food through BananaNow.

And so, the jungle's very own food delivery service was born!
Within minutes orders poured in.
Monkey started working nonstop.

Elephant and Giraffe ordered veggie burgers to enjoy by the river.

Monkey kept right on working.

Zebra and her friends wanted some popcorn delivered so they wouldn't miss their favorite series, *A Million Stripes*.

Monkey kept right on working.

Beetle club ordered fresh elephant dung to be delivered nightly.

Monkey kept right on working.

The ants ordered wheat: four thousand three hundred and twenty-three grains, to be exact. One for each of them. Count them out, count them out...

Monkey kept right on working.
And with all that hustle, he was getting rich!

But he was getting more and more worn out.

He missed the simple life: eating a banana or a pineapple from time to time and splashing around in the river with his friend Hippo.

Despite his exhaustion, Monkey continued delivering everyone's orders quickly and with no complaints.

Until the day an order came in from Lion.

"I'm having a dinner party with all my lion friends, and we'd like five servings of monkey with rice."

Right then and there, Monkey decided that he was going to shut down BananaNow forever. He sent out a message to all his customers, and to Lion, too.

Monkey disconnected all of BananaNow's computers, keyboards, tablets, and phones.

And then he headed down to the river to kick back for a while, singing a little tune as he went...

A SWIM WITH MY BUDDY BEATS RICHES, YOU SEE,

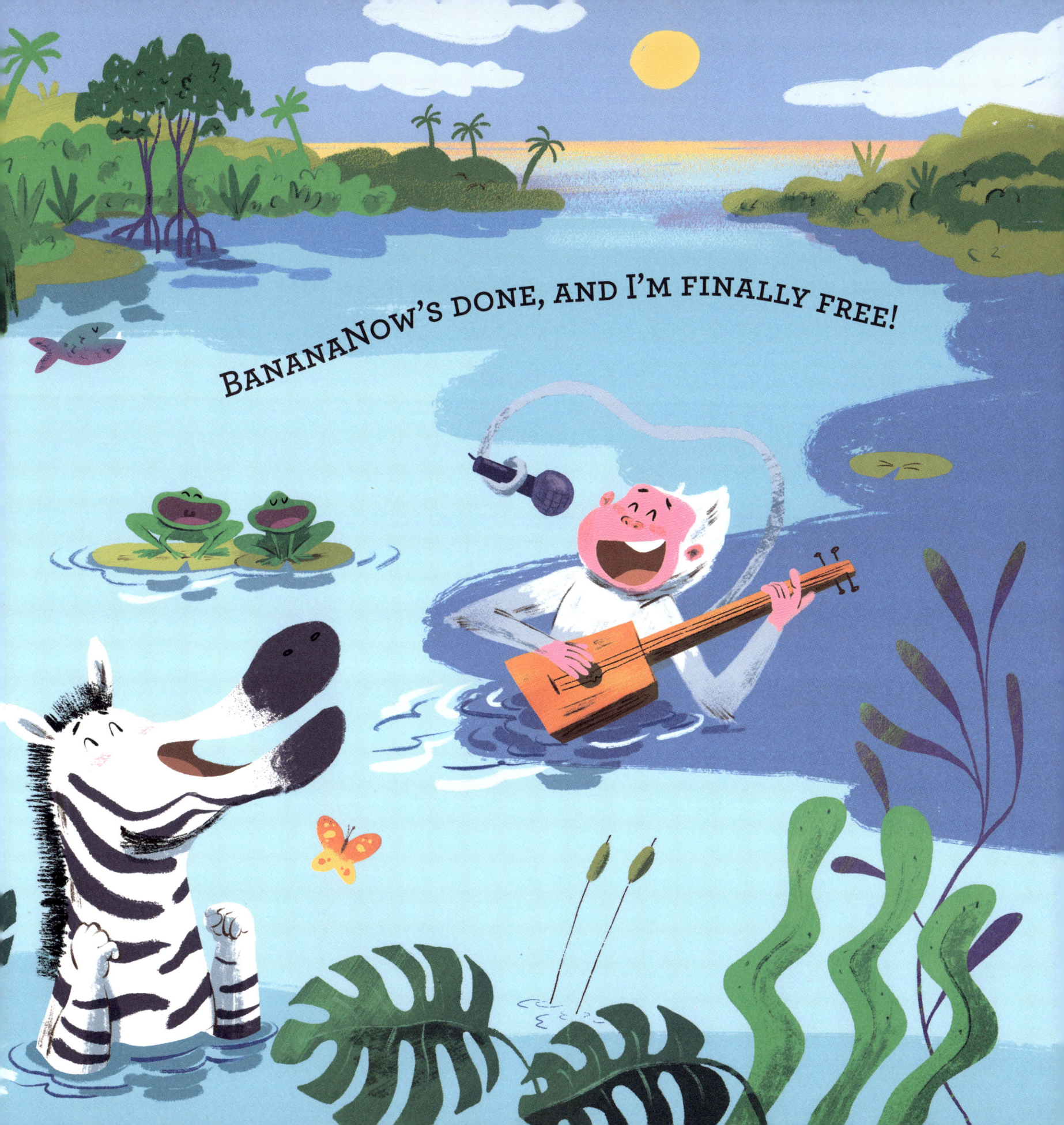